Aesop's Fables

for Little Children

These stories were first
told a long, long time ago.
Each of them has a moral,
or lesson, about life.

Aesop's Fables
for Little Children

From the stories by Aesop
Illustrated by John Joven
Retold by Susanna Davidson

Contents

The Hare and the Tortoise

Moral: Slow and steady wins the race.

It was Spring, beautiful Spring!
And Hare was off... run, run, running!

She was *fast* as the wind
and light as the breeze.

"I can run all day...

"...and into the night. I can even touch
the moon!" she laughed.

Look at me!

"I'm *faster* than EVERYONE!" boasted Hare. "And as *for* you, Old Mr. Tortoise... well, there's no contest, is there!"

You just plod, plod, plod.

How RUDE.

"Humph!" thought Tortoise, in a grump. "Someone needs to teach that Hare a lesson!"

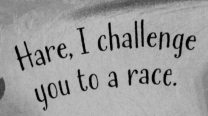

Hare, I challenge you to a race.

Tortoise! Are you crazy?

Word got around *fast*. On the day
of the race, everyone *flocked* to watch.
No one thought Tortoise stood a chance...

We'll race from here
to the oak tree
and back.

"Are you ready?"
hooted Owl.
"Are you steady?

On your marks...

Get...

Set...

...GO!"

And they were off! Hare dashed
away in a blur of pale fur.
Tortoise took one... slow... step.

In a matter of minutes, Hare reached the oak tree. "Well," she sighed. "This is dull. Where's the competition?"

It's tough being so great.

"I think I'll take a little nap."
And she lay down on the warm grass.

In no time at all,
Hare was *fast* asleep.

She woke only as the sun began to set,
and the birds were settling down to rest.

The race!
The Race!

Hare heard the
animals at the *finish*
line, cheering *for* Tortoise.
She leaped to her *feet*.

She ran *faster* than the wind, *faster* than the river...

...up hill and down dale...

But she was
TOO LATE!

There was Tortoise, inching towards the finish.

Noooooo!

The next moment, it was all over.
Tortoise was THE WINNER!

Well done, Tortoise!

Three cheers
for Tortoise!

"But... I'm the *fastest!*" panted Hare.
"Tortoise can't be the winner!"

This isn't
fair!

Better luck next time, Hare.

Tortoise grinned. "You see, my friend," he said, "slow and steady wins the race."

The Lion and the Mouse

Moral: Little friends
can be great friends.

The midday sun was high in the sky over the African grasslands.

Chief Mouse mopped his brow.
"Time to go home," he declared.

It's far too
hot for me.

Chief Mouse led
everyone back to the
burrow, but Little Mouse
couldn't keep up.

Oh dear!
Where has
everyone gone?

Soon, she was all alone in the grasslands...
and *feeling* rather afraid.

"I'm lost," she called.
"Is there anybody there?"
But no one answered.

Then, in the distance, she spied a hill.
"I know," thought Little Mouse.
"If I climb that hill, I'll be able to see
where I am."

Up I go!

...and higher.

...and higher...

And so up she went, higher...

She couldn't help thinking that it was a very strange hill. It was soft and *fluffy*, and it seemed to be moving.

"Maybe it's not a hill at all?" thought Little Mouse. "But if it's not a hill... WHAT *is* it?"

It's a
LION!

The lion was
fast asleep.
Unfortunately,
Little Mouse
squeaked so
loudly, the lion...

...WOKE UP!

"How **DARE** you wake
me?" the lion snarled.

I'm very sorry.

It was an accident.

43

Little Mouse tried to run away, but
Lion caught her by the tail.

"Do you know what I do to those
who wake me?" said the Lion.

"I EAT them."

Little Mouse gulped.

"I'm much
too small to
eat," said
Little Mouse.

"And I
don't think
I taste very
nice."

"WAIT!
I have
AN IDEA!
And it's a
good one!"

Lion waited, Little Mouse
dangling from his jaws.

"If you save my life today,"
said Little Mouse,
"then, one day, I'll save yours."

How Lion laughed! "YOU could never save ME! But because you made me laugh, I'll let you go."

"You will not regret this decision. I PROMISE," said Little Mouse.

Back in her burrow, Little Mouse
told the other mice her story.
"How could **YOU** ever save a Lion?"
they laughed. "You're the smallest of us all."

But Little Mouse ignored them.
"You'll see," she said. "You'll see."

That very night, the lion walked
straight into a hunter's trap.

He roared and he clawed,
but there was no way out.

The more he *fought*, the **tighter**
the trap became.

Deep in her burrow, Little Mouse
heard Lion's roars.

Roarrrrrrrrr!

"I must go to him,"
she thought. "Lion
needs me."

"I promised I would help him, and mice keep their promises."

Then Little Mouse ran, following the roars that echoed through the darkness.

At last, she found Lion,
caught fast in a net.

"There's nothing you can do," said Lion, sadly.

But Little Mouse began to gnaw at the ropes. She nibbled and gnawed all through the night.

By dawn, the lion was *free*.
"Thank you, Little Mouse," he said.

"I see, now, that little *friends*
can be great *friends*, after all."

The Fox and the Crow

Moral: Don't be
fooled by flattery.

Once there was
a Fox who loved...
CHEESE!
And, one day, he
spied a delicious
yellow chunk of it.

"How I WANT
that cheese,"
he thought.

There was just one problem...
the cheese belonged to Crow.

But I can
make it mine.

Fox tried **very** hard
to reach the cheese...

Nearly there...

If I can just....

But, as everyone knows,
foxes can't climb trees.

Fox wasn't one to give up easily.
"There must be a way to get that cheese!"

All I need is a
cunning plan...

"You'll never do it," said Squirrel.
"No one can outwit Crow."

"That's right," whispered Bear. "Crow will never *fall* for your tricks."

"Have you ever seen a *fox* outfoxed?" said Fox. "I know EXACTLY what to do."

On those words,
Fox sauntered
over to Crow.

"How delightful it is
to see you," called Fox.
"What a beautiful
bird you are!"

"You have such glossy black feathers," purred Fox.

"Oh I do," thought Crow, proudly. "I really do."

It was time for
the finale. The
pièce de résistance.
"Dear Crow," begged
Fox. "How I would love
to hear you sing...

...after all, such a
beautiful bird must
have a beautiful voice!"
cooed Fox.

"Me? Sing?" wondered Crow. "I always thought my voice was a little... croaky?"

Bear and Squirrel chuckled to themselves. "Everyone knows crows can't sing!"

"Oh Crow..." oozed Fox.

"If you can sing as well as I think, then you would truly be RULER OF THE BIRDS!"

Crow thought about it. "RULER OF
THE BIRDS! I like the sound of that.
Yes! I'd make a wonderful ruler!"

All the other birds could wait on me.

I could wear a velvet cloak and a crown!

And so, with beak open wide, Crow
began to sing... CAW! CAW! CAW!

As for the cheese... down it fell...

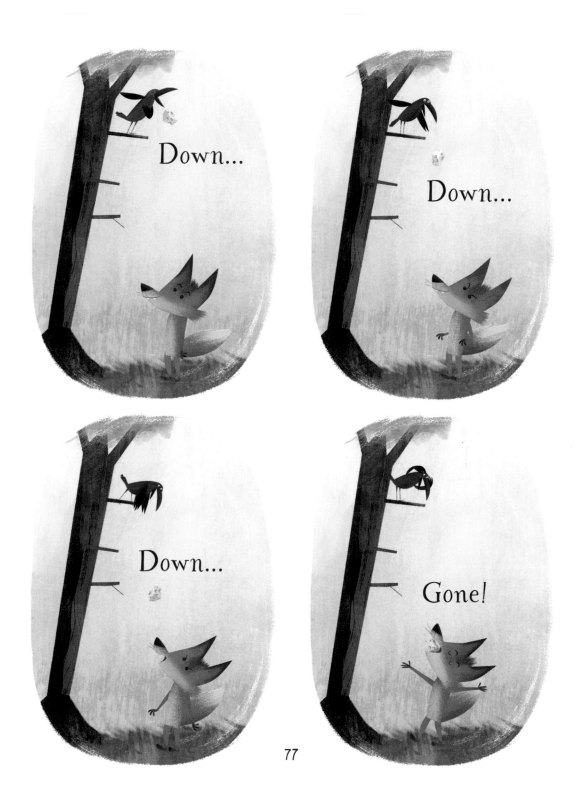

77

Fox guzzled it all in one gulp.

Delicious...
scrumptious...
delumptious!

"Crows can't sing!" mocked Fox. "And a real ruler would never fall for that trick!"

"I'll never be fooled
by flattery again,"
snapped Crow, flying
away in a fury.

"But," Crow vowed,
"I've learned my
lesson from this!"

Crow flew
on, until...

"Ah! Hello, Mouse. I've heard what a wise and wonderful mouse you are. I'd love to hear you talk..."

Moral: Prepare for
winter before it comes.

The Ant and the Grasshopper

The sun was shining,
the bees were buzzing and
Grasshopper was singing.

Fiddle-dee-dum! Fiddle-dee-dee!
I'm as happy as can be...

Riddle-dee-dum! Riddle-dee-dee!
This is the perfect life for me!

87

As Grasshopper sang, Ant worked. "Who's got time to sing?" she muttered as she ran by. "Busy, busy, busy – that's me!"

"I can't stop!" spluttered Ant.

"So much to do! So little time!"

Ant
hurried and
scurried...

...this way and
that, never
stopping for a
moment's rest.

"But what are you DOING?"
asked Grasshopper, puzzled.

"I'm collecting food for winter," huffed Ant.

"YOU should be doing the same."

"Who cares about winter? It's ages away!" scoffed Grasshopper.

"Come and sing with me!"

Fiddle-dee-dum!
Fiddle-dee-dee!

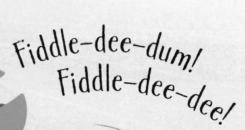

"Winter will come," called
Ant, as she hurried away,
"and then you'll be sorry..."

Grasshopper took no notice of Ant's warning. He sang the summer away.

The days passed in a heady blur of warm breezes and blue skies.

Grasshopper
sang to the swifts
and the swallows.
He sang to
the butterflies
and bees.

When he
saw Ant, he
felt pity for
her wasted
summer.

But soon, the days began
to shorten. A faint chill
nipped at the air.

First the swifts left, and
then the swallows.

They swooped and dived for the last
time through the summer skies.

"Where are you going?"
asked Grasshopper.

"To Africa," the
swallows replied.
"In search of
the sun."

Then the last of the petals
fell from the flowers.

The wind whipped
the leaves from the trees.

There was no food left.
The corn was gone
from the field, and the
hedgerows grew silent.

What will I do now?

One morning,
Grasshopper
woke to beautiful
white flakes,
drifting down
from the sky.

But they *fell*
thick and *fast*.
Grasshopper
could find no
warmth.

"If only I'd worked all summer, like Ant," thought Grasshopper. "If only I could have my time again."

Grasshopper curled up under a leaf, and tried to sleep.

He was woken by someone calling.

"You'll never last the
winter out here," said Ant.

"I have *food* and a warm
fireside," Ant said.

Ant led Grasshopper down twisting, turning tunnels...

...deep into the warm dark earth.

Welcome to
my home!

After supper, Grasshopper made
Ant a promise. "Next year, I'll work
hard all summer."

"Now I know,
prepare for
winter before
it comes!"

"And I'll sing
while we work!"
laughed Ant.

Fiddle-dee-dum!
Fiddle-dee-dee!

The Fox and the Stork

Moral: Treat others as you
would like them to treat you.

Fox was a trickster,
no doubt about it.
And what Fox loved
most of all was
to play tricks on
his friends.

Today, he
decided, it was
Stork's turn.
So he wrote a
letter, inviting
Stork to supper.

Stork was
DELIGHTED
to receive the
invitation...

...and spent **ALL
DAY** getting
ready, choosing
the very best hat
to wear. (Stork
loved hats.)

By the time Stork set out, the wind was howling, and the rain was pouring. But Stork didn't want to let Fox down.

An hour later, a very soggy Stork arrived at Fox's house.

"Come inside!" said Fox. "I've made us some soup."

Fox poured the soup into wide, shallow bowls. Stork was so excited.

It smelled wonderful!

"It's my best soup yet," said Fox,
gulping it down.
"So tasty!"

Stork tried very hard
to eat the soup...

...but it was
IMPOSSIBLE!

Fox began to laugh.

"You tricked me!"
cried Stork. "You're
supposed to be
my friend!"

Stork strutted home through the rain.
"I'm going to get that Fox..."

All night, Stork stayed awake,
determined to come up with a plan.
At last, he had it!

I know exactly
what I'm going to do!

At once, Stork sat down to write Fox a letter, inviting him to supper.

Fox was **DELIGHTED** to receive the invitation. "Stork is an amazing cook. I can't wait!"

Fox hardly ate a mouthful **ALL DAY**, so he would have plenty of room in his tummy for Stork's delicious supper...

"I've made stew," said Stork.
"I hope you like it."

"I can't wait!" chuckled Fox.
"I'm *famished.*"

Stork poured the
soup into tall jars.
Fox did everything
he could to eat
the soup...

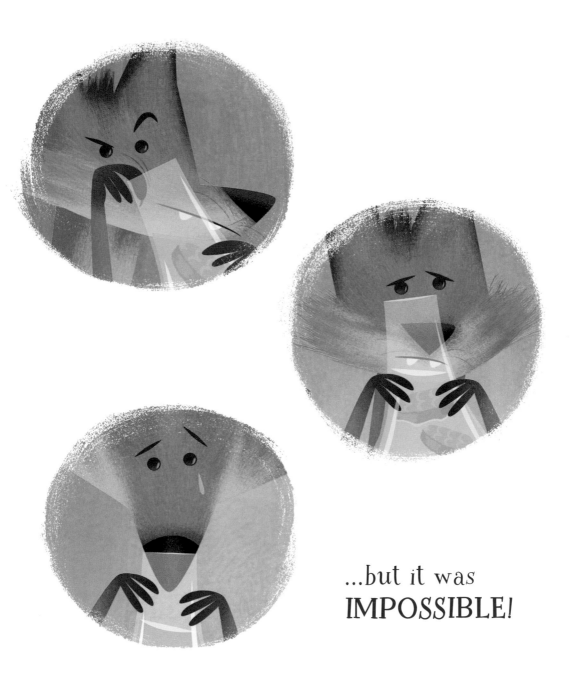

...but it was
IMPOSSIBLE!

As for Stork... how he laughed!

"You tricked me!" snapped the furious Fox. "You shouldn't play tricks on your friends."

"Well," said Stork, "you tricked **ME** first. Now you know how it feels."

For the first time ever, Fox felt terrible about all the tricks he had played on his friends.

The next day, he hurried to Stork's house. "I'm so sorry," he said. "I'll never play tricks on my friends again."

Will you come to my house for lunch?

The Town Mouse and the Country Mouse

Moral: There's no place like home.

Town Mouse LOVED town life.
Every night, he played with his band,
Town Mouse and the Rat-a-tat-tats.

"But lately," Town Mouse confessed to his friend, "I've been feeling a little... bored!"

RATS AND JAZZ

MILKSHAKE BAR

"What you need," said his friend, "is a change of scene. Why not take a trip?"

Town Mouse decided to visit his
cousin in the country. He set off
the very next morning.

Chugga-chugga-chugga
went the train. **Choo! Choo!**

Town Mouse arrived as the light faded, and the stars began to shine. "Ah!" he said. "So peaceful and quiet!"

Then he
stepped in a
cow splat...

...and came
face to face
with a cow.

At last, he arrived at his cousin's house. "Surprise!" he cried. "Cousin, I've come to stay!"

Country Mouse was overjoyed. "Come inside," she said. "We'll celebrate with a *feast*!"

Country Mouse laid out
her best nuts and berries.

"Call this a *feast*?"
thought Town Mouse.

The next morning, Town Mouse
was woken early by a very loud...

COCK-A
DOODLE
DOOOOOO!

"What a dreadful racket!" thought Town
Mouse. "So much for peace and quiet."

"I know!" said Country Mouse. "We'll go for a picnic by the stream. You'll love it!" But Town Mouse was not **at all** sure of the company.

It's a monster!

It's only a dragonfly.

Nor did Town Mouse enjoy the swim...

146

"I can't take this any more," said Town Mouse. "I **HAVE** to go home."

"Why don't you come and stay in town with me?"

"Really?" said Country
Mouse. "I'd love to!
I've never been
to town before."

They set off that very night. Town Mouse took Country Mouse straight to the best restaurant in town.

"We'll feast on blue cheese!" said Town Mouse. But Country Mouse missed her nuts and berries.

After supper,
Town Mouse
sang with
his band...

"My poor
ears!" thought
Country
Mouse. "It's
so... **LOUD!**"

In bed that night, Country Mouse couldn't sleep. Cars raced past the window.

Vroom! Vroom! Vroom!

And the blue cheese had given her tummy ache.

"I miss my home," said Country Mouse. "I know it's simple, but it's right *for* me."

"But there's so much more to see!" cried Town Mouse.

"Do you really have to go?"

"We're each better in our own homes,"
said Country Mouse.

So Town Mouse took his cousin to
the station and waved goodbye.

Country Mouse walked home in the starry dark. She sniffed the cold, fresh air, and smiled.

"Country Mouse!" called her friend,
Hedgehog. "How was your trip?"

"Come to my house for berry tea,"
said Country Mouse. "And I'll tell
you all about it..."

"Well?" said Hedgehog.
"It was new and strange and exciting," said Country Mouse.

Designed by Vickie Robinson
Edited by Lesley Sims
Digital imaging: John Russell

First published in 2020 by Usborne Publishing Ltd., Usborne House, 83-85 Saffron Hill,
London EC1N 8RT England, usborne.com Copyright © 2020, 2019 Usborne Publishing Ltd.
The name Usborne and the devices ♀ ⊕ are Trade Marks of Usborne Publishing Ltd.
All rights reserved. No part of this publication may be reproduced, stored in a retrieval system, or
transmitted in any form or by any means, electronic, mechanical, photocopying, recording
or otherwise without the prior permission of Usborne Publishing Ltd. First published
in America 2020, UE, EDC, Tulsa, Oklahoma 74146 usbornebooksandmore.com